STRESS MANAGEMENT

Learn to Relax

Dr. R. Dhananjayan

DISCOVERY PUBLICATIONS

No. 9, Flat No. 1080A, Rohini Flats,
Munusamy Salai, K.K. Nagar (West),
Chennai - 600 078. Mobile: 99404 46650

STRESS MANAGEMENT

Dr. R. Dhananjayan©

First Edition: DEC - 2022

DP-0222

ISBN No : 978-93-95285-31-5

Pages: 40

Publisher • *Sales Rights*

Discovery Publications	**Discovery Book Palace (P) Ltd**
No. 9, Plot,1080A, Rohini Flats, Munusamy Salai, K.K.Nagar West, Chennai - 600 078. Mobile: +91 99404 46650	No. 1055-B, Munusamy Salai, K.K.Nagar West, Chennai-600 078. Contct: +91 87545 07070

discoverybookpalace@gmail.com

WWW.DISCOVERYBOOKPALACE.COM

Please download the 'Discovery Book Palace' App and scan the QR Code to buy a copy of this book.

Preface

We are born to live happily with peace of mind. But there are many factors which decide our day-to-day life to be happy or sad. Most of the time our happiness depends on how we lead a life and how we handle various situations. In our life we need to face stressful situations also. Stress is a normal psychological and physical reaction to demands of life. If a small amount of stress motivates us, it's good, but in excess, if challenges for a longer period beyond our coping capacity, it is dangerous. Sometimes stress may results anxiety, which is a feeling of fear, worry or unease. The stress and anxiety have identical symptoms. Even though naturally we have fight-or-flight mechanism to deal the stress, the unmanaged stress and anxiety interferes with daily life and spoil our mental and physical health.

Stress has powerful impact on various aspects of our life, not only affecting our mood, energy level, relationships and work performance, it can also affect health. So stress has negative impact on health, relationships, job and day-to-day performances including personal life. It is common to experience the stress and in the same way there are many strategies to manage it. Effective stress management helps us to cope with stress and so that we can be happier, healthier and more productive. We can lead a balanced life with time for work, relationships, relaxation and fun. Preventing and managing long-term stress lowers the risk for conditions like, heart disease, obesity, high blood pressure and depression.

Along with my profession I had the opportunity to take stress management sessions using hands-on techniques to doctors and healthcare workers of various units of Apollo Hospitals, Chennai, and to the employees of few companies, i.e., BDP International, Hyundai Motor Company etc. For these sessions I am grateful to our Training and Marketing Department of Apollo Hospitals, Chennai. This journey created me a platform to discuss with people on various aspects of stress and also to understand how they deal the common and uncommon stressful situations in their daily life. I could observe that the stress differs from person to person and few were able to cope and few were not.

The feedback of my sessions gave a clear picture that the practice of stress management techniques in long run yields good results for building mental health. These sessions help people to analyze the factors causing and triggering the stress and to minimize its harmful effects. It is very important to choose specific stress management strategy which fits the individual. Based on my experience I have written this book. This book mainly focuses on the background of stress and the ways to cope with stress using various practical techniques. Hope this book helps everyone to lead happy and peaceful life by managing the stress.

Dr. R. Dhananjayan
doctordhananjayan@gmail.com

December, 2022

Content

STRESS

What is Stress?

There are easy and difficult situations in our day-to-day life. Success and failure are the part of life. We celebrate the successes, but don't even digest the failures. The stress is experienced when there is failure to respond intellectual, emotional or physical demands, whether actual or imagined. Stress is an automatic physical, mental and emotional response to a challenging event.

Many of us find difficult to cope with the emotional and physical demands brought about by stressful situations. The situations and factors cause stress are known as stressors. So stress is physical, cognitive and emotional reaction of the body to stressor or situations that demand change.

The stress differs from person to person and situation to situation. The way we respond to stress makes a big difference to our overall well-being. According to World Health Organization (WHO) the stress is manifested as fear, worry, inability to relax, increased heart rate, difficulty in breathing, disturbance in sleeping patterns, change in eating patterns, difficulty in concentrating, worsening of pre-existing health conditions (physical and mental) and increased use of alcohol, tobacco and other drugs.

Types

(1) Eustress

It is a good stress, which motivates us to work harder and makes us feel energetic.

E.g., winning in a competition, getting academic achievement, getting promotion in a job etc

(2) Distress

When a stress produces the feeling of being overwhelmed and other harmful effects causes distress. It may be due to external or internal factors.

E.g., External factors – financial problems, relationship issues etc; Internal factors – health issues, way of thinking etc

Depending on the situation, stress can have positive or negative effect. A little amount of stress motivates us for development. But if it is more, causes health issues.

Causes for Stress

- ❖ Change in environment
- ❖ Lack of individual attention
- ❖ No time management
- ❖ Inadequate sleep
- ❖ Improper diet
- ❖ Distractions

- ❖ Conflicts
- ❖ Expectations
- ❖ Peer pressure
- ❖ Relationship issues
- ❖ Health issues
- ❖ Financial issues
- ❖ Conflicts
- ❖ Failures

Effect of stress on the body

In all stressful situations, hypothalamus in brain is activated and results in same type of symptoms. The sympathetic nervous system is activated, which activates the central parts of the adrenal glands, releasing the hormones epinephrine and norepinephrine. These hormones are responsible for increased heart rate, blood pressure, elevated respiratory rate, muscle tension, etc.

A sequence of physiological reactions takes place when a person faces a stressor known as 'General Adaptation Syndrome'. It is a three-stage process. It describes the undergoing processes of body when exposed to any kind of stress, positive or negative. Even after this, if the stress is not reduced, it can lead to physical and mental health problems.

General Adaptation Syndrome (GAS)

It has the following stages,

> (1) The Alarm Stage
> (2) The Resistance Stage
> (3) The Exhaustion Stage

(1) The Alarm Stage

In this stage, the body recognizes the stress and mobilizes all resources to deal with the stressor. The body starts secreting the hormones like epinephrine and prepares itself to fight or evade the situation. Heart and respiratory rates increase, muscles are tensed, digestion slows down and the body on the whole gets ready for action. If the problem is solved, the body gets back to normal and if not forges to next stage.

(2) The Resistance or The Adaptation Stage

If a person faces a stressor for a long time, his / her body tries to resist or adapt to the stressor, known as Resistance or the Adaptation stage. If the body does not adapt to the stressor, it enters to next stage.

(3) The Exhaustion Stage

When the mind and body cannot cope with extreme or prolonged stress, enter the final stage known as the Exhaustion Stage. All energy gets depleted and the person becomes vulnerable to experience more distress.

The Nervous System and Stress Response

The stress is responded by autonomic nervous system and hypothalamic-pituitary-adrenal (HPA) axis.

The sympathetic nervous system controls 'fight or flight' response and the parasympathetic nervous system controls 'rest and digest' response.

The functions of sympathetic and parasympathetic branches oppose and complement each other to create balance and maintain homeostasis.

The activation of stress response stimulates the HPA axis to produce the hormone cortisol into the blood, which mobilizes stored glucose, fat and amino acids to support the energy needed to cope with the stressor.

The release of hormones norepinephrine and epinephrine provides an immediate start to the stress response and the stimulation of HPA axis and release of cortisol provide fuel to sustain response till the stressor is resolved.

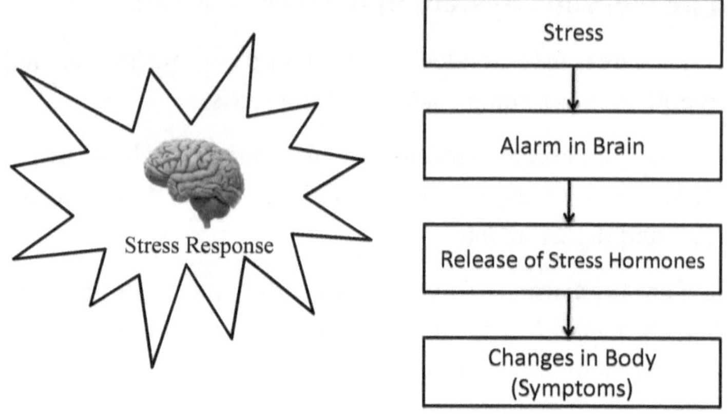

Fig. 1: Stress Response

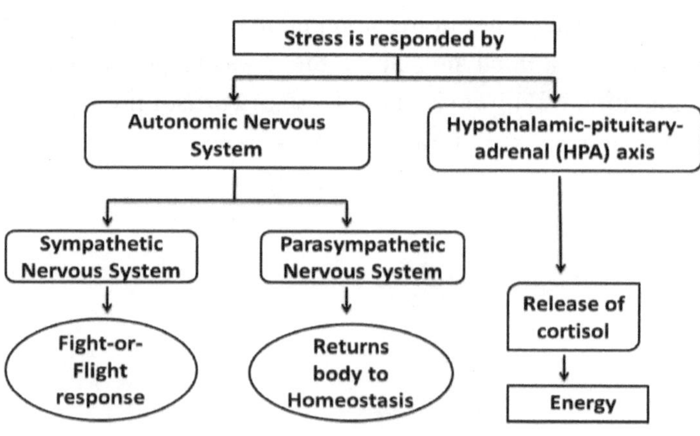

Fig. 2: Role of Nervous System

Acute and Chronic Stress

Acute Stress

It is a short term stress exists for a short duration. Once the problem is solved, the body is back to normal and relaxed. The body can handle episodes of acute stress and can recover quickly. The blood pressure, heart rate, breathing rate and levels of muscle tension may be abnormal for a short while and comes back to normal.

Examples include any stress suffer from for a short period of time - stuck in a traffic jam, argument with a person etc.

Chronic Stress

It is a long-term stress exists for long duration. Experiencing stress for a long time results in various physical and psychological problems. The body cannot easily handle chronic stress. It creates new normal inside the body, which leads to health problems including high blood pressure, heart disease, chronic pain, depression etc. To deal with chronic stress, coping skills with relaxation techniques are to be practiced on regular basis.

Examples include the acute stress which can turn into chronic stress - stuck in numerous traffic jams a day, constant argument with a person etc

Signs of Stress

The stress can create lot of feelings such as fear, anger, depression, restlessness, irritability, insecurity, confusion etc.

Long term stress has the impact on immune system and contributes to developing various physical and psychological illnesses.

The signs of stress are divided into

(1)   Physical Signs

(2)   Cognitive Signs

(3)   Emotional Signs

(4)   Behavioural Signs

1. Physical Signs

- Headache
- Fatigue
- Breathlessness
- Sweating
- Shivering
- High BP
- Dry mouth
- Stomach-churning
- Racing heart
- Cold hand and feet

2. Cognitive Signs

- ❖ Negative thinking
- ❖ Worry about minor matters
- ❖ Indecisiveness
- ❖ Poor Attention and Concentration

3. Emotional Signs

- ❖ Low self confidence
- ❖ Anxiety
- ❖ Depression
- ❖ Irritation on minor issues
- ❖ Sadness

4. Behavioural Signs

- ❖ Restlessness
- ❖ Loss of appetite
- ❖ Loss of sleep
- ❖ Accident - prone
- ❖ Drinking alcohol
- ❖ Smoking
- ❖ Avoidance of situations
- ❖ Criticism
- ❖ Denial
- ❖ Escape
- ❖ Violence
- ❖ Aggression

Why stress management is important?

Stress management is the range of techniques, strategies and therapies used to control stress. It is used to reduce the acute stress, but also aimed to reduce chronic stress to improve health, happiness and overall well-being by improving mental health. It is important for the following,

- ❖ To cope with stress
- ❖ To reduce the risk of associated conditions such as heart diseases, obesity, high blood pressure and depression
- ❖ To deal with stress and difficulty in life
- ❖ To lead a balanced and healthy life

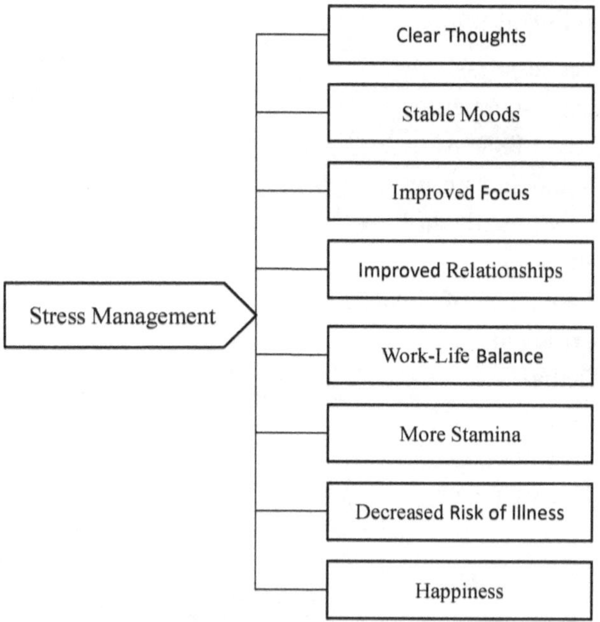

Fig. 3: Importance of Stress Management

QUALITIES TO BE DEVELOPED TO MANAGE STRESS

(a) Personal Development

Developing Good Habits

Habits are the acts or behaviour we do repeatedly, so that they become automatic. The habits which are beneficial for self and others are known as good habits. The habits which are harmful for self or others are known as bad habits.

Good Habits

- ❖ Regular sleep routine
- ❖ Disciplined life
- ❖ Punctuality
- ❖ Reading good books
- ❖ Having positive attitude
- ❖ Healthy eating
- ❖ Regular physical activity

How to develop a habit?

- ❖ Practice consistently
- ❖ Deal with one habit at a time
- ❖ Write it down
- ❖ Take help of family and friends
- ❖ Just do it
- ❖ Reward yourself

How to get rid of bad habits?

- ❖ Make a list of bad habits
- ❖ Set a realistic goal
- ❖ Take help of family and friends
- ❖ Find substitute / Replacement of bad habits
- ❖ Have patience
- ❖ Get rid of bad habits one by one

(b) Self-Confidence

It is the key to success. It is the confidence in oneself and in one's abilities. If you are confident, you believe that you have the ability to deal with challenges and problems.

How to improve Self-Confidence?

- ❖ Walk straight, keep body posture properly
- ❖ Have smile on your face
- ❖ Identify your uniqueness and be proud
- ❖ Identify and overcome the weaknesses
- ❖ Identify and strengthen the strengths
- ❖ Keep fit, exercise regularly,
- ❖ Consume nutritious and balanced diet
- ❖ Wear neat clothes

❖ Help others
❖ Be positive
❖ Learn from others, experience and surroundings

(c) Interpersonal Relations

We feel happy and relaxed when we are with the people whom we like. We are healthier and happier with good friends and family members. Family and friends support is very important to lead a healthy life. Poor social relations also cause stress. Sharing our feelings with our well-wishers helps to reduce our stress. Making and maintaining relationships is an important aspect of life.

(d) Handling the Conflicts

A conflict is a difference between two or more beliefs, ideas or interests, which leads to an argument and fight. Consider the following to handle the conflicts.

❖ Understand from others perspective
❖ Have realistic expectations
❖ Avoid comparisons
❖ Communicate properly
❖ Pause the discussion when you are in anger/upset
❖ Empathize
❖ Think about your contribution to the problem
❖ Listen to emotions
❖ Negotiate
❖ Have kindness
❖ Talk to each other
❖ Ignore small irritating issues
❖ Learn to tolerate
❖ Accept the limitations
❖ Be non-judgemental
❖ Be honest and genuine

- ❖ Have self-regulation
- ❖ Do not avoid
- ❖ Be balanced

(e) Handling the Failures

Success and failure are part of life. Everyone would have faced failure at any point at least once. If a person is not able to reach his / her desired goal or not able to get positive results, he / she considers it as failure. It is a matter of perception. It is always better to consider failure as an opportunity to make another attempt for achieving the goal.

Consider the following to handle the failures.

- ❖ Accept
- ❖ Analyze
- ❖ Change the strategy
- ❖ Give extra efforts
- ❖ Share the feelings with well-wishers and seek help
- ❖ Avoid comparisons
- ❖ Believe your ability
- ❖ Be optimistic

COPING SKILLS

A situation is less stressful, if we have enough resources to deal with it. It is always good to have optimism, resilience, good communication skills, good interpersonal relations, problem solving skills etc. The coping strategies are,

(1) Problem – Focused Coping

It is based on solving the problem by working on finding the solutions and implementing them. Indecisiveness, procrastination, lack of confidence, knowledge and guidance are the causes of poor problem solving.

The strategies to be used are,

- ❖ Identify the problem and do root-cause using "W" questions, i.e., What, When, Where and Who?
- ❖ Have an achievable goal
- ❖ Have, analyze and choose the alternatives
- ❖ Implement the solution
- ❖ Fix the target
- ❖ Monitor the progress
- ❖ Accept the problem and find solution to cope
- ❖ Take social support

(2) Emotion – Focused Coping

It is used when the situations are not under our control and which are not going to change. It helps to accept the problems we are facing. If it is used for long period, may not be useful. It is useful when the stress is at its initial stage.

The strategies to be used are,

- ❖ Distraction
- ❖ Denial – refusing to believe the stressful situation
- ❖ Scheduling the worry time
- ❖ Journaling
- ❖ Meditation
- ❖ Acceptance
- ❖ Praying / Being spiritual
- ❖ Humour
- ❖ Vent the emotions

EMOTIONAL QUOTIENT (EQ)

It is also known as Emotional Intelligence. It is the ability to understand, use and manage our own emotions in positive ways to relieve stress, communicate effectively, empathize with others, overcome challenges and defuse conflict

Characteristics of Low Emotional Quotient

- ❖ Aggressive
- ❖ Demanding
- ❖ Egotistical
- ❖ Unresponsive
- ❖ Being Slow
- ❖ Stubborn
- ❖ Fussy
- ❖ Blaming Others
- ❖ Being Argumentative

Characteristics of High Emotional Quotient

- ❖ Assertive
- ❖ Ambitious
- ❖ Determined
- ❖ Decisive
- ❖ Enthusiastic
- ❖ Predictable
- ❖ Consistent
- ❖ Stable
- ❖ Good Listening

Emotional intelligence helps

- ❖ To build stronger relationships
- ❖ To succeed at work
- ❖ To achieve your career and personal goals
- ❖ To connect with your feelings
- ❖ To make informed decisions

The key skills to build EQ and improve your ability to manage emotions are,

(1) **Self-management** – Manage your emotions in healthy ways, take initiative, follow through on commitments and adapt to changing circumstances

(2) **Self-awareness** – Recognize your own emotions and aware that how they affect your thoughts and behaviour. Know your strengths and weaknesses and have self-confidence.

(3) **Social awareness** – Have empathy. Try to understand the emotions, needs and concerns of other people.

(4) **Relationship management** – Communicate clearly, inspire and influence others, work as a team and learn to manage conflicts.

RELAXATION TECHNIQUES

There are many relaxation techniques to manage the stress. The following are few such exercises. Learn properly and practice on regular basis for healthy and peaceful mind.

(1) Muscle Relaxation Technique

(2) Yoga and Power Yoga

(3) Mindfulness Meditation

(4) Exercise

(5) Pranayama

(6) RECBT

1. Muscle Relaxation Technique

Jacobson's relaxation technique is a therapy focuses on tightening and relaxing specific muscle groups in sequence. It's also known as Progressive Muscle Relaxation (PMR) Therapy. It was found by American physician Edmund Jacobson in the 1920s. It was based on the theory that physical relaxation can promote mental relaxation. The technique involves tightening one muscle group while keeping rest of the body relaxed, and then releasing the tension.

Benefits

- Relieves anxiety and tension
- Reduces work-related stress
- Lowers blood pressure
- Eases neck pain
- Reduces low back pain
- Improves sleep

How to do it?

It can be done by lying or sitting down.

- Relax the entire body
- Close your eyes
- Have normal breathing by concentrating on breathe for 2 minutes

❖ Do the following steps, step by step individually for fingers, eyes, jaws, head, stomach and toes.

    1) Tighten

    2) Normal Breathing for 8 Seconds

    3) Slow Release

    4) Feel the Relaxed Stage

    5) Have relaxing Deep Breath Twice

❖ Now tightening the fingers, eyes, jaws, head, stomach and toes, all together at a time, repeat the above steps once.

❖ Have normal breathing by concentrating on body for 2 minutes.

❖ Slowly move body parts and gently open the eyes.

It can also be done for muscles of other body parts, i.e., knees, thighs, hands, chest, shoulders, lips, mouth etc.

2. Yoga and Power Yoga

Yoga

Yoga is a series of stretches and poses doing with breathing techniques. It is an ancient practice originated in India. It is a system of exercises for body that involves breath control and helps to relax both mind and body.

The modern yoga is a posture-based physical fitness, stress-relief and relaxation technique, consisting largely of the asanas, differs from traditional yoga, which focuses on meditation and release from worldly attachment. Both are for mind and body practice.

It involves movement, meditation and breathing techniques to promote mental and physical well-being. It is used to build strength, awareness and harmony in both the mind and body. It improves strength, balance and flexibility. Slow movements and deep breathing increase blood flow and warm up muscles while holding a pose can build strength.

It offers the powerful benefits of exercise. Since yoga is gentle, anyone can do it, regardless of age or fitness level.

Yoga should not be performed in a state of exhaustion, illness, in a hurry or in an acute stress conditions. Women should refrain from regular yoga practice especially asanas during their menses. It works on the level of one's body, mind, emotion and energy.

Benefits

- ❖ Improves strength, balance and flexibility
- ❖ Benefits heart health
- ❖ Improves sleep
- ❖ Helps to manage stress
- ❖ Promotes better self-care

Power Yoga

It is a fast-paced style of yoga that's focused on building strength and endurance. It is also an excellent form of yoga for burning calories

It enhances stamina, flexibility, posture and mental focus. It relieves stress and burns more calories.

The main difference between yoga and power yoga is the speed of practice. In yoga you move body parts slowly and maintain steady flow and a structured rhythm. But power yoga is carried out quicker than regular yoga.

3. Mindfulness Meditation

Meditation is a simple practice, which is beneficial to reduce stress, increase calmness, improve sleep and to promote happiness. The beginners have to start with guided meditations from experienced teacher.

Mindfulness meditation is based on paying attention to the present moment with an accepting, nonjudgemental disposition.

There is no need for stop thinking or empty the mind. Pay close attention to physical sensations, thoughts and emotions in order to see them more clearly, without making assumptions.

Mindfulness is the experience of being open and aware of present moment without judgement, automatic criticism or mind wandering.

Meditation is the training of attention which cultivates that mindfulness. It can be practiced at any time of the day, but preferably in the morning.

How to practice?

- ❖ Choose a comfortable place

- ❖ Take your seat comfortably (Sitting or any comfortable position)

- ❖ Straighten but don't stiffen the upper body

- ❖ Close your eyes (not mandatory)

- ❖ Relax. Bring attention to breath or sensations in the body

- ❖ Feel the breath - draw attention to physical sensation of breathing: the air moves through nose, the rising and falling of belly or chest. Choose a focal point and with each breath, you can mentally note 'breathing in' and 'breathing out'.

- ❖ No need to block or eliminate thinking. If the mind wanders, in few seconds or minutes just gently return attention to the breath. Even if it is wandering continuously try to come back over and over again without judgement or expectation.

- ❖ About 5 to 10 minutes it can be practiced. Once if it is over, gently open your eyes (if they are closed). Notice the sounds in the environment. Notice how the body feels? Notice the thought and emotions.

4. Exercise

Physical activity improves your body's ability to use oxygen and also improves blood flow. Both of these changes have a direct effect on your brain. Physical activity activates the release of a neurotransmitter called dopamine, which improves mood. Regular exercises improve superior cognitive function and emotional well being.

Exercises are effective to deal with and handle stress and anxiety. It also stimulates the production of endorphins, chemicals in the brain that are the body's natural painkillers and mood elevators. Regular exercise, every day or three times a week, encourages brain to regularly release endorphins which can help to improve the mood.

Exercise reduces levels of the body's stress hormones, such as adrenaline and cortisol. The release of endorphins combined with the reduction of stress hormones helps to feel calm.

Running, cycling and swimming are all different forms of cardio exercise which are good for heart and lungs. Cardio exercises can be done in the morning (so the day starts with the release of endorphins) which are most effective in stress management.

Regular aerobic exercise will bring remarkable changes to the body, metabolism, heart and spirits. It has a unique capacity to exhilarate and relax, to provide stimulation and calm, to counter depression and dissipate stress.

Using large muscle groups in rhythmic, repetitive fashion work-outs are also the best. It is also known as muscular meditation. E.g., walking and jogging.

5. Pranayama

It is the practice of breath regulation. It is an ancient breathing technique for physical and mental wellness. In Sanskrit, 'prana' means life energy and 'yama' means control. It involves controlling the breath in different styles and lengths. It has three phases,

    (1) Inhalation
    (2) Retention
    (3) Exhalation

Benefits

- Improves cognitive functions
- Improves lung function
- Helps in stress and emotional regulation
- Significantly lowers anxiety levels and any negative feelings associated with it
- To manage psychosomatic disorders
- Improves concentration
- Improves blood circulation
- Relieves stress, depression and hypertension
- Releases anxiety
- Builds self-confidence
- Develops positive thinking
- Used to calm and center the mind
- Brings the mind to present moment
- Helps to harmonize the left and right hemispheres of the brain, which correlates to logical and emotional sides of our personality (alternate nostril breathing)
- Maintains body temperature

How to practice Pranayama (Alternate nostril breathing)?

- ❖ Sit straight, be comfortabe and let shoulders be relaxed
- ❖ Keep left hand on left knee and palms open to sky (or chin mudra – thumb and index finger gently touching at the tips)
- ❖ Keep the tip of index finger and middle finger of the right hand in between eyebrows.
- ❖ Keep the ring finger and little finger on left nostril and thumb on right nostril. Use them to open and close the respective nostrils.
- ❖ Close right nostril and breathe out through left nostril and then breathe in from the same nostril. Now close left nostril and breathe out throught right nostril and then breathe in from the same nostril. Exhale from left. This is one round. It is recommended to complete 9 rounds

Note:

- ❖ After every exhalation, breathe in from same nostril
- ❖ Close the eyes during pranayama
- ❖ Take long, deep, smooth breaths without any force of effort

Where to do?

- ❖ At a clean environment and with full of fresh air

When to do?

- ❖ Morning or Evening, preferably in the morning
- ❖ When you wake up in the morning drink two glasses of water and go for a walk and then do pranayama

Dos

- ❖ Empty Stomach for better results
- ❖ Practice Regularly: Only regular practice can give you better results

Don't

- ❖ Do not eat before Pranayama
- ❖ Women should not practice yoga during menstrual days
- ❖ Pregnant women should not practice few pranayama, (where you hold breath for long time/ exhale)

6. RECBT (Rational Emotive Cognitive Behaviour Therapy)

* ❖ It helps to resolve emotional, behavioural problems and disturbances
* ❖ Used to change irrational beliefs to rational beliefs
* ❖ Used to overcome anxiety and phobias
* ❖ Improves interpersonal relationship
* ❖ Changes negative thought and emotions to positive outcomes

Try to give your Answer for the following questions (as per RECBT)

Q. No.	Question	If the Answer is
1	Is there 100 % evidence for my thought / Belief ?	No
2.	Does my thought helps me to solve problem?	No
3.	Is my thought is a conditional statement?	Yes
4.	Is my expectation completely in my control ?	No

Interpretation

Compare your answer and the given answer. If the given answer arrives even for one of the questions, then it is irrational behavior. So do not get emotionally disturbed by unfortunate circumstances.

TIPS TO MANAGE THE STRESS

1. Observe Yourself - Identify Stress Triggers

- ❖ Vague pain
- ❖ Tight muscle
- ❖ Stomach upset
- ❖ Fatigue
- ❖ Disturbed sleep
- ❖ Anxiety
- ❖ Things out of your control
- ❖ Observe thought, mood and emotion

2. Relax – Bring Nervous system back to balance

- ❖ Deep breathing
- ❖ Yoga
- ❖ Meditation
- ❖ Practice any relaxation technique regularly

3. Unplug - Spend Less Time in front of Screen – TV, Computer, Tab, Phone etc.

4. Do Rhythmic Activity – Walking, Cycling, Dancing, Aerobics

5. Healthy Diet

- ❖ Eat Balanced diet
- ❖ Maintain regular meal timing
- ❖ Don't skip meals

6. Peaceful Rest and Recreation

> ❖ Have Regular Sleep – Go to Bed at same time

7. Connect and Bond with others – Share the feeling with your well – wishers

8. Engage your Senses

> ❖ Sight – Have a look on the things you like
> ❖ Sound – Listen to songs / music
> ❖ Taste – Have the balanced diet
> ❖ Smell – Can use aroma and be fresh
> ❖ Touch – Have decent hug

9. Work- Life Balance – Give equal priority to the demands of career and the demands of personal life

10. Reframing - Reframing is a way that we can alter our perceptions of stressors (Think out of the Box)

11. Be optimistic – Be positive

12. Don't multitask - Juggling many tasks at the same time is stressful

13. Spend one hour per day for you on things you like

14.Time Management – Plan and divide the time for activities

15. Give importance to priority

Draw your clock as follows and give priority accordingly,

- ❖ Urgent and Important
- ❖ Important but not urgent
- ❖ Urgent but not important
- ❖ Neither important nor urgent

The Stress…

Let it

be

the reason

for Motivation!

not for

Depression!!

Manage the Stress… Lead a Peaceful Life